**Favorite Uncle Wiggily Animal Bedtime Stories**

HOWARD GARIS

With a new introduction by
Brooks Garis
*Uncle Wiggily Classics, Inc.*

*Illustrated by Thea Kliros*

DOVER PUBLICATIONS, INC.
Mineola, New York

# DOVER CHILDREN'S THRIFT CLASSICS
## EDITOR OF THIS VOLUME: ADAM FROST

### Bibliographical Note

This Dover edition, first published in 1998, is a new selection of fifteen stories reprinted from *Uncle Wiggily and Sammie and Susie Littletail,* A. L. Burt Company, New York, 1910. The introductory Note and the illustrations by Thea Kliros have been prepared specially for this edition.

### Library of Congress Cataloging-in-Publication Data

Garis, Howard Roger, 1873–1962.
    Favorite Uncle Wiggily animal bedtime stories / Howard Garis.
       p.     cm.
    "Introductory note and the illustrations by Thea Kliros have been prepared specially for this edition"—Copyr. p.
    Summary: Fifteen favorite bedtime stories relate the adventures of the gentleman rabbit, his Littletail family, Jane Fuzzy-Wuzzy, and others.
    ISBN 0-486-40101-4 (pbk.)
    [1. Rabbits—Fiction.  2. Animals—Fiction.]  I. Kliros, Thea, ill. II. Garis, Howard Roger, 1873–1962.  Uncle Wiggily and Sammie and Susie Littletail.  III. Title.
PZ7.G182Fav   1998
[E]—dc21                                         97–42202
                                                CIP
                                                AC

Manufactured in the United States of America
Dover Publications, Inc., 31 East 2nd Street, Mineola, N.Y. 11501

# Uncle Wiggily and the Newspapers:
## The Adventures of Howard R. Garis
### by Brooks Garis

In the early days of this century, America's powerful city papers were the heart and soul of communication. America was in love with the high speed of the written word and virtually every household received at least one paper a day.

My grandfather, Howard R. Garis, was part of this world. He worked as a reporter on the *Evening News* in Newark, New Jersey, but in the evenings, after his day's work as a reporter was completed, he was a writer of adventure stories under various pen names for the famous syndicator of juvenile literature, Edward L. Stratemeyer.

My grandmother, Lilian Garis, was also a writer and the first newspaper woman in New Jersey. She joined Howard in "ghosting" for Stratemeyer, and together with their two grown children—my father Roger, and his sister Cleo—they became a family of four word-crafters who were dubbed "The Writing Garises" in a 1934 article in *Fortune Magazine*. They penned dozens of popular series: all but the last two volumes of the *Tom Swift* classics, most of the *Bobbsey Twins,* all of the *Baseball Joe* series and many others, a total of over 500 titles.

E. M. Scudder, publisher of the *Evening News,* knew the real hand behind *Tom Swift* and asked my grandfather if he would write some children's stories for the paper, possibly about animals, to run, perhaps, four weeks. My grandfather said he would think about it.

Out for a walk one day and wondering what to write, Howard Garis spotted a rabbit with long, wiggily ears, making his home in a hollow stump. That afternoon, Uncle Wiggily was born, and within a few weeks Uncle Wiggily Longears was hopping off the presses and into the homes of thousands, and eventually millions of children everywhere.

There was a new "Uncle Wiggily Bedtime Story" every working day, six stories a week, and each one ended with a humorous little closing that set the mind spinning and told the title of the next story to come. The *Evening News* had become the first paper anywhere to hand-deliver a serialized bedtime story just in time for Moms and Dads to read their youngsters off to sleep.

The stories were soon running in daily papers around the country and beyond. The tales were amusing and adventurous but not frightening, and the characters had delightful names and charming expressions. Children loved them.

The daily syndication of Uncle Wiggily continued for nearly fifty years, and along the way there were hundreds of books, toys, and the still-popular Uncle Wiggily Game. Shortly before my grandfather died in 1962, he asked my mother, also a writer, to carry on the Uncle Wiggily stories—and so they continue today.

Brooks Garis
Uncle Wiggily Classic, Inc.

# Contents

*This was a family of bunny rabbits.*

## Sammie Littletail in a Trap

ONCE UPON a time there lived in a small house built underneath the ground two curious little folk, with their father, their mother, their uncle and Jane Fuzzy-Wuzzy. Jane Fuzzy-Wuzzy was the nurse, hired girl and cook, all in one, and the reason she had such a funny name was because she was a funny cook. She had long hair, a sharp nose, a very long tail and the brightest eyes you ever saw. She could stay under water a long time, and was a fine swimmer. In fact, Jane Fuzzy-Wuzzy was a big muskrat, and the family she worked for was almost as strange as she was.

There was Papa Littletail, Mamma Littletail, Sammie Littletail, Susie Littletail and Uncle Wiggily Longears. The whole family had very long ears and short tails; their eyes were rather pink and their noses used to twinkle, just like the stars on a frosty night. Now you have guessed it. This was a family of bunny rabbits, and they lived in a nice hole, which was called a burrow, and which they had dug under ground in a big park on the top of a mountain, back of Orange. Not the kind of oranges you eat, you know, but the name of a place, and a very nice place, too.

1

In spite of her strange name, and the fact that she was a muskrat, Jane Fuzzy-Wuzzy was a very good cook and quite kind to the children bunnies, Sammie and Susie. Besides looking after them, Jane Fuzzy-Wuzzy used to sweep the burrow, make up the beds of leaves and grass, and go to market to get bits of carrots, turnips or cabbage, which last Sammie and Susie liked better than ice cream.

Uncle Wiggily Longears was an elderly rabbit, who had the rheumatism, and he could not do much. Sometimes when Jane Fuzzy-Wuzzy was very busy he would go after the cabbage or turnips for her. Uncle Wiggily Longears was a wise rabbit, and as he had no other home, Papa Littletail let him stay in a warm corner of the burrow. To pay for his board the little bunnies' uncle would give them lessons in how to behave. One day, after he had told them how needful it was to always have two holes, or doors, to your burrow, so that if a dog chased you in one, you could go out of the other, Uncle Wiggily said:

"Now, children, I think that is enough for one day, so you may go out and have some fun in the snow."

But first Jane Fuzzy-Wuzzy looked out of the back door, and then she looked out of the front door, to see that there were no dogs or hunters about. Then Sammie and Susie crept out. They had lots of fun, and pretty soon, when they were quite a ways from home, they saw a hole in the ground. In front of it was a nice, juicy cabbage stalk.

"Look!" cried Sammie. "Jane Fuzzy-Wuzzy must have lost that cabbage on her way home from the store!"

"That isn't the door to our house," said Susie.

"Yes it is," insisted Sammie, "and I am going to eat the cabbage. I didn't have much breakfast, and I'm hungry."

"Be careful," whispered Susie. "Uncle Wiggily Longears

*"Oh, Susie! Something has caught me by the leg!"*

warned us to look on all sides before we ate any cabbage we found."

"I don't believe there's any danger," spoke Sammie. "I'm going to eat it," and he went right up to the cabbage stalk.

But Sammie did not know that the cabbage stalk was part of a trap, put there to catch animals, and, no sooner had he taken a bite, than there came a click, and Sammie felt a terrible pain in his left hind leg.

"Oh, Susie!" he cried out. "Oh, Susie! Something has caught me by the leg! Run home, Susie, as fast as you can, and tell Papa!"

Susie was so frightened that she began to cry, but, as she was a brave little rabbit girl, she started off toward the underground house. When she got there she jumped right down the front door hole, and called out:

"Oh, Mamma! Oh, Papa! Sammie is caught! He went to bite the cabbage stalk, and he is caught in a horrible trap!"

"Caught!" exclaimed Uncle Wiggily Longears. "Sammie caught in a trap! That is too bad! We must rescue him at once. Come on!" he called to Papa Littletail, and, though Uncle Wiggily Longears was quite lame with the rheumatism, he started off with Sammie's papa, and to-morrow night I will tell you how they saved the little boy rabbit.

## Sammie Littletail Is Rescued

WHEN UNCLE Wiggily Longears and Papa Littletail hurried from the underground house to rescue Sammie, Mamma Littletail was much frightened. She nearly fainted, and would have done so completely, only Jane Fuzzy-Wuzzy brought her some parsnip juice.

"Oh, hurry and get my little boy out of that trap!" cried Mamma Littletail, when she felt better. "Do you think he will be much hurt, Uncle Wiggily?"

"Oh, no; not much," he said. "I was caught in a trap once when I was a young rabbit, and I got over it. Only I took a dreadful cold, from being kept out in the rain all night. We will bring him safe home to you."

While Uncle Wiggily Longears and Papa Littletail were on their way, poor Sammie, left all alone in the woods, with his left hind foot caught in a cruel trap, felt very lonely indeed.

"I'll never take any more cabbage without looking all around it, to see if there is a trap near it," he said to himself. "No indeed I will not," and then he tried to get out of the trap, but could not.

Pretty soon he saw his father and his uncle coming over the snow toward him, and he felt much better.

"Now we must be very careful," said Uncle Wiggily Longears, to Papa Littletail. "There may be more traps about."

So he sat up on his hind legs, and Papa Littletail sat up on his hind legs, and they both made their noses twinkle like stars on a very frosty night. For that is the way rabbits smell, and these two were wise bunnies, who could smell a trap as far as you can smell perfumery. They could not smell any traps, and they could not see any with their pink eyes, so they went quite close to Sammie, who was held fast by his left hind leg.

"Does it hurt you very much?" asked his papa, and he put his front paws around his little rabbit boy, and gave him a good hug.

"Not very much, Papa," replied Sammie, "but I wish I was out."

"We'll soon have you out," said Uncle Wiggily Longears, and then with his strong hind feet he kicked away the snow and dried leaves from the trap. Then Sammie could see how he had been fooled. The trap was so covered up that only the cabbage stump showed, so it is no wonder that he stepped into it.

The two rabbits tried to get Sammie out, but they could not, because the trap was too strong.

"What shall we do?" asked Papa Littletail, as he sat down and scratched his left ear, which he always did when he was worried about anything.

"The trap is fast to a piece of wood by a chain," said Uncle Wiggily Longears. "We will have to gnaw through the wood, and then take Sammie, the trap, chain and all, home. Once there, we can call in Dr. Possum, and he can open the trap and get Sammie's leg out."

So the two big rabbits set to work to gnaw through the wood, to which the chain of the trap was fastened. Sammie Littletail tried not to cry from the pain, but

*The two rabbits tried to get Sammie out.*

some tears did come, and they froze on his face, close
to his little wiggily nose, for it was quite cold.

"I should have given you a lesson about traps," said
Uncle Wiggily Longears; "then perhaps you would not
have been caught. I will give you a lesson to-morrow."

Finally the wood was gnawed through, and Sammie,
with his uncle on one side and his papa on the other, to
help him, reached home. The trap was still on his leg,
and he could not go very fast. In fact, the three of them
had to go so slow that a hunter and his dog came after
them. They managed, however, to jump down the hole

of the underground house just in time, and the big dog did not get them. He soon got tired of waiting, and went away. Then Dr. Possum was sent for, and with his strong tail he quickly opened the trap, and Sammie was free. But his leg hurt him very much, and Jane Fuzzy-Wuzzy put him in a bed of soft leaves and gave him some sassafras and elderberry tea. Dr. Possum told Sammie he would have to stay in the burrow for a week, until his leg was better. Sammie did not want to, but his mother insisted on it, and to-morrow night I will tell you an adventure that happened to Susie Littletail, when she went to the store for some cabbage.

## What Happened to Susie Littletail

IT WAS very lonesome for Sammie Littletail to stay in the underground house for a whole week after he had been caught in the trap. He had to move about on a crutch, which Uncle Wiggily Longears, that wise old rabbit, gnawed out of a piece of cornstalk for him.

"Oh, dear, I wish I could go out and play!" exclaimed Sammie one day. "It's awfully tiresome in here in the dark. I wish I could do something."

"Would you like a nice, juicy cabbage leaf?" asked Susie.

"Wouldn't I, though!" cried Sammie. "But there isn't any in the pantry. I heard Jane Fuzzy-Wuzzy tell mother so."

"I'll go to the store and get you some," offered his sister. "I know where it is."

The cabbage store was a big field where Farmer Tooker kept his cabbage covered with straw during the winter. It was not far from the burrow, and, though it was not really a store, the rabbits always called it that. So that was where Susie Littletail went. She scraped the snow off the straw with her hind feet and kicked the straw away so she could get at the cabbage. Then she began to gnaw off the sweetest leaves she could find for her little sick brother. She had broken off quite a number and was thinking how nice they would be for him, when she suddenly smelled something strange.

It was not cabbage nor turnips nor carrots that she smelled. Nor was it sweet clover, nor any smell like that. It was the smell of danger, and Susie, like all her family, could smell danger quite a distance. This time she knew it was a man with a dog and a gun who was

*A man with a dog and a gun was coming toward her.*

coming toward her. For Uncle Wiggily Longears had told her how to know when such a thing happened.

"Oh, it's some of those horrid hunters; I know it is!" exclaimed Susie. "I must run home, though I haven't half enough cabbage."

She took the leaves she had gnawed off in her mouth and bounded off toward the underground house. All at once a dog sprang out of the bushes at her and the man with the gun shot at her, but he did not hit her. She was so frightened, however, that she dropped the cabbage leaves and ran for her life.

Oh, how Susie Littletail did run! She never ran so fast before in all her life, and, just as the dog was going to grab her, she saw the back door of her house, and into it she popped like a cork going into a bottle.

"Oh! Oh! Oh!" she cried three times, just like that. "I am safe!" and she ran to where her brother was, on a bed of leaves.

"Why, Susie!" he called to her. "Whatever is the matter?"

"Yes. Why have you been running so?" asked Jane Fuzzy-Wuzzy. "What happened?"

"A big dog chased me," answered Susie. "But I got away."

"Where is my cabbage?" Sammie wanted to know. "I am so hungry for it."

"Oh, I'm so sorry, but I had to drop it," went on Susie. "Oh, Jane Fuzzy-Wuzzy, is Papa home safe? Where is Uncle Wiggily Longears? I hope neither of them is out, for I'm afraid that hunter and his dog will see them."

"Your uncle is asleep in his room," said the muskrat nurse. "His rheumatism hurts him in this weather. As for your papa, he has not come home yet, but I guess he is wise enough to keep out of the way of dogs. Now don't make any noise, for your mamma is lying down with a headache. I have a little preserved clover, done up in sugar, put away in the cupboard, and I will give you some."

"That is better than cabbage," declared Sammie, joyfully.

But, just as Jane Fuzzy-Wuzzy went to the cupboard to get the sugared clover, something ran down into the underground house. It was a long, thin animal, with a sharp nose, sharper even than Jane Fuzzy-Wuzzy's, and when the nurse saw the curious little beast, she cried out in fright:

"Oh, run, children! Run!" she screamed. "This is a very dreadful creature indeed! It is a ferret, but I will drive him out, and he shan't hurt you!"

Then Nurse Jane Fuzzy-Wuzzy, dropping the pan of potatoes she was peeling for supper, sprang at the ferret. And to-morrow night, if you are good children, you shall hear how Jane Fuzzy-Wuzzy drove the ferret from the underground home and saved the bunny children.

## Papa Littletail's Picture

WHEN NURSE Jane Fuzzy-Wuzzy called out to the two bunny children to run away from the ferret, Sammie and Susie were so frightened that they hardly knew what to do. Their mother came into the sitting-room of the burrow, from the dark bedroom where she had gone to lie down, because of a headache, and she also was much alarmed. So was Uncle Wiggily Longears, who was awakened from his nap by the cries of the nurse.

"Run and hide! Run and hide!" called Jane Fuzzy-Wuzzy, and all the rabbits ran and hid. The ferret, which was a long, slender animal, something like a white rat, had been put into the burrow by the hunter, who stood outside at the back door, hoping the rabbits would run out so he could shoot them. But they did not. Instead, they went into the darkest part of the underground house. Nurse Jane Fuzzy-Wuzzy went bravely up to the ferret.

"Now you get right out of this house," she said. "We don't want you here!"

The ferret said nothing, but kept crawling all around, looking for the rabbits. He was careful to keep away

13

*"Now will you go?" asked the nurse.*

from the muskrat, for, in spite of her soft name, Nurse Jane Fuzzy-Wuzzy had very sharp teeth.

"Come on, now; get right out of here!" the nurse said again, but the ferret would not go. He wanted to catch the rabbits. Then the muskrat jumped right up on his back and bit him quite hard on one of his little ears. The ferret squealed at this.

Next Jane Fuzzy-Wuzzy nipped him on the other ear; not very hard, you know, but just hard enough to make that ferret wish he had stayed out of the underground house.

"Now will you go?" asked the nurse.

"Yes," said the ferret, "I will," and he turned around

and walked right out of the house. The hunter was very much surprised when his ferret appeared without having driven out any rabbits. He could not understand it.

"Well," he said, "I guess I made a mistake, but I was sure I saw a rabbit go down that hole. I guess I had better be going." So he called his dog, put his ferret into his pocket and went away. And, oh, how glad Sammie and Susie Littletail were!

Pretty soon Papa Littletail came hurrying home. As soon as he entered the burrow the children noticed that he was rather pale. He said that he had had a terrible fright, for, as he was on his way home from Mr. Drake's house, a boy had pointed a big, black thing at him, which clicked like a gun, but did not make a loud noise. Then Susie told him about the dog who chased her, and how the ferret had frightened them.

"It is a good thing you were not shot," said Mamma Littletail to her husband. "I don't know what we would have done if such a dreadful thing had happened. How terrible boys are!"

"I did have a narrow escape," admitted Papa Littletail. "The boy had a sort of square, black box, and I'm sure it was filled with bullets. It had a great, round, shiny eye, that he pointed at me, and, when something clicked, he cried out, 'There, I have him!' But I did not seem to be hurt."

"I know what happened to you," said Uncle Wiggily Longears, and he rubbed his leg that had the worst rheumatism in it. "You had your picture taken; that's all."

"My picture taken?" repeated Papa Littletail, as he scratched his left ear, which he always did when he was puzzled.

"That is it," said the children's uncle. "It happened to me once. The boy had a camera, not a gun. It does not hurt to have your picture taken. It is not like being shot."

"Then I wish all hunters would take pictures of us, instead of shooting at us," said Sammie, and Susie also thought it would be much nicer. And Uncle Wiggily told how lovers of animals often take their pictures, to put in books and magazines, for little boys and girls to look at.

"Well," said Papa Littletail, "I suppose I should be very proud to have my picture taken, but I am not the least bit."

Then he gave Sammie some nice pieces of chocolate-covered turnip, which Mr. Drake had sent to the little boy with the lame leg.

"Do you think I can get out to-morrow?" asked Sammie, after supper. "My leg is quite well."

"I think so," replied his papa. "I will ask Dr. Possum."

Which he did, and Sammie was allowed to go out. He had a very curious adventure, too, and I think I shall tell you about it tomorrow night, if you go to bed early now.

## Sammie Littletail Digs a Burrow

SAMMIE LITTLETAIL found that his leg was quite well enough to walk on, without the cornstalk crutch, so the day after his papa's picture had been taken, the little rabbit boy started to leave the burrow.

"Come along, Susie," he called to his sister.

"I will also go with you," said Uncle Wiggily Longears. "I will give you children a few lessons in digging burrows. It is time you learned, for some day you will want an underground house of your own."

So he led them to a nice place in the big park on top of the mountain, where the earth was soft, and showed Sammie and Susie how to hollow out rooms and halls, how to make back and front doors, and many other things a rabbit should know.

"I think that will be enough of a lesson to-day," said Uncle Wiggily Longears, after a while. "We will go home, now."

"No," spoke Sammie, "I want to dig some more. It's lots of fun."

"You had better come with us," remarked Susie.

But Sammie would not, though he promised to be home before dark. So while Uncle Wiggily Longears and

Susie Littletail started off, Sammie continued to dig. He dug and he dug and he dug, until he was a long distance underground, and had really made quite a fine burrow for a little rabbit. All at once he felt a sharp pain in his left fore leg.

*"What do you mean by digging into my house?"*

"Ouch!" he cried. "Who did that?"

"I did," answered a little, furry creature, all curled up in a hole in the ground. "What do you mean by digging into my house? Can't you see where you are going?"

"Of course," answered Sammie, as he looked at his sore leg. "But couldn't you see me coming, and tell me to stop?"

"No, I couldn't see you," was the reply.

"Why not?"

"Why not? Because I'm blind. I'm a mole, and I can't see; but I get along just as well as if I did. Now, I suppose I've got to go to work and mend the hole you made in the side of my parlor. It's a very large one." The mole, you see, lived underground, just as the rabbits did, only in a smaller house.

"I'm very sorry," said Sammie.

"That doesn't do much good," spoke the mole, as she began to stop up the hole Sammie had made. She really did very well for a blind animal, but then she had been blind so long that she did not know what daylight looked like. "You had better dig in some other place," the mole concluded, as she finished stopping up the hole.

Sammie thought so himself, and did so. He went quite deep, and when he thought he was far enough down, he began digging upward, so as to come out and make a back door, as his uncle had taught him to do. He dug and he dug and he dug. All at once his feet burst through the soft soil, and he found that he had come out on top of the ground. But what a funny place he was in! It was not at all like the part of the park near his burrow, and he was a little frightened. There were many tall trees about, and in one was a big gray squirrel, who sat up and chattered at the sight of Sammie, as if he had never seen a rabbit before.

"What are you doing here?" asked the squirrel. "Don't you know rabbits are not allowed here?"

"Why not?" asked Sammie.

"Because there are nice trees about, and the keepers

of the park fear you and your family will gnaw the bark off and spoil them."

"We never spoil trees," declared Sammie, though he just then remembered that his Uncle, Wiggily Longears, had once said something about apple-tree bark being very good to eat.

"There's another reason," went on the squirrel, chattering away.

"What is it?" asked Sammie.

"Look over there and you'll see," was the reply, and when Sammie looked, with his little body half out of the hole he had made, he saw a great animal, with long horns, coming straight at him. He tried to run back down the hole, but he found he had not made it large enough to turn around in.

So Sammie Littletail, frightened as he was at the dreadful animal, had to jump out of the burrow to get ready to run down it again, and, just as he did so, the big animal cried out to him:

"Hold on there!"

Sammie shook with fright, and did not dare move. But, after all, the big animal did not intend to harm him. And what happened, and who the big animal was I will tell you to-morrow night.

## Sammie and Susie Help Mrs. Wren

THE BIG animal with the horns came close to Sammie. "What are you doing here?" he asked.

"I—I don't know," replied the little rabbit boy.

"How did you get here?"

"I was digging a new burrow, and I—I just happened to come out here. But I'll go right away again, if you'll let me."

"Of course I'll let you. Don't you know it's against the rules of the park to be here? What do you suppose they have different parts of the park for, if it isn't to keep you rabbits out of certain places?"

"I'm sure I don't know," was all Sammie could say.

"Do you know who I am?" asked the horned creature.

"No—no, sir."

"Well, I'm a deer."

"My—my mother calls me that, sometimes, when I've been real good," said Sammie.

"No, I don't mean that kind at all," and the deer tried to smile. "My name is spelled differently. I'm a cousin of the Santa Claus reindeer. But you must go now. No rabbits are allowed in the part of the park where we live.

21

You should not have come," and the deer shook his horns at Sammie.

"I—I never will again," said the little rabbit boy, and then, before the deer knew it, Sammie jumped down his new burrow, ran along to the front door, and darted off toward home.

When he was almost there he saw a little brown bird sitting on a bush, and the bird seemed to be calling to him.

"Wait a minute, rabbit," said the bird. "Why are you in such a hurry?"

"Because I saw such a dreadful animal," was Sammie's reply, and he told about the deer.

"Pooh! Deer are very nice creatures indeed," said the bird. "I used to know one, and I used to perch on his horns. But what I stopped to ask you about was whether you know of a nice nest which I could rent for this spring. You see, I have come up from the South a little earlier than usual, and I can't find the nest I had last year. It was in a little wooden house that a nice man built for me, but the wind has blown it down. I didn't know but what you might have seen a little nest somewhere."

"No," said Sammie, "I haven't. I am very sorry."

"So am I," went on the little brown bird. "But I must tell you my name. I am Mrs. Wren."

"Oh, I have heard about you," said the little rabbit.

"Are you sure you don't know of a nest about here?" she asked anxiously. "I don't want to fly all the way back down South. Suppose you go home and ask your mother."

"I will," said Sammie. "Don't you want to come, too?"

"Yes, I think I will. Oh, dear! I'm quite hungry. I declare, I had such an early breakfast, I'm almost starved."

"I know my mother will give you something to eat,"

said Sammie politely, "that is, if you like cabbage, carrots and such things."

"Oh, yes, almost anything will do. Now, you go ahead, and I will follow."

So Sammie Littletail bounced on along the ground, and Mrs. Wren flew along overhead.

"Where do you live?" she asked Sammie.

"In a burrow."

"What is a burrow?" she inquired

"Why, it's a house," said Sammie.

"You are mistaken," said the bird, though she spoke politely. "A nest is the only house there is."

"Well, a burrow is our house," declared Sammie. "You'll see."

He was soon home, and, while the bird waited outside, he went in to ask his mother if she knew of a nest Mrs. Wren could hire.

"What a funny question!" said Mamma Littletail. "I will go out and see Mrs. Wren."

So she went out, and the bird asked about a nest. But, as the rabbits never had any use for them, the bunny knew nothing about such things.

"Oh, dear!" exclaimed the bird. "Wherever shall I stay to-night? Oh, what trouble I am in."

"You might stay with us to-night," said Mamma Littletail, kindly, "and look for a nest to-morrow."

"I never lived in a burrow," said Mrs. Wren, "but I will try it," so she flew down into the underground house, and to-morrow night I am going to tell you how she did a great kindness to Uncle Wiggily Longears.

## Uncle Wiggily Gets Shot

EARLY THE next morning Mrs. Wren, who had spent the night at the home of the Littletail family, got up. She had some cabbage leaves for her breakfast, and then started to leave the burrow where the rabbits lived.

"Where are you going?" asked Susie Littletail.

"I must go hunt for a nest," said the little bird. "You see, I want to begin housekeeping as early as I can this spring, and as there are so many birds coming up from the South, I want to get a house before all the best ones are taken."

So, having thanked Sammie Littletail for showing her the way to the burrow, and also thanking his mamma and papa, the bird flew away. She promised, however, to come back if she could not find a place.

"That Mrs. Wren is a very nice creature indeed," said Mamma Littletail.

"Indeed she is," agreed Papa Littletail, as he started off to work in the carrot store, where he was employed as a bookkeeper.

"It is a nice day," said Uncle Wiggily Longears, after a while. "I think I will go for a walk. It may do my rheumatism good."

24

*Uncle Wiggily was running as hard as he could.*

"Can I come?" asked Sammie, but his uncle said he thought the little boy rabbit should stay at home. So Sammie did, and he and Susie found a place where some nice clover was just coming up in a field.

Just before dinner time Uncle Wiggily Longears came limping back to the burrow. He was running as hard as he could, but that was not very fast.

"Why, Wiggily, whatever has happened?" asked Mrs. Littletail, who had come to the front door to see if her children were all right. "Is your rheumatism worse? Why do you limp so?"

"Because," answered Uncle Wiggily Longears, "I have been shot."

"Shot?" cried Mrs. Littletail.

"In the left hind leg," went on Uncle Wiggily. "The same leg that has the rheumatism so bad. Oh, dear! I wish you would send for Dr. Possum."

"I will, right away. Sammie!" she called, "come and go for Dr. Possum, for your uncle. He has been shot. How did it happen, Wiggily?"

"Well, I was down in the swamp, looking for some snakeroot, which Mr. Drake said was good for rheumatism, when a man fired at me. I jumped, but not in time, and several pieces of lead are in my leg."

"Oh, how dreadful!" cried Mamma Littletail.

In a little while Sammie came back with Dr. Possum.

"Ha! This is bad business," spoke the long-tailed doctor, when he looked at Uncle Wiggily Longears's leg. "I fear I shall have to operate."

"Anything, so you get the shot out," said the old rabbit.

So Dr. Possum tried to get the leaden pellets out, but he could not, they were in so deep.

"This is very bad business, indeed," he went on. "I fear I shall have to take your leg off." ·

"Will it hurt?" asked Uncle Wiggily Longears.

"Um-er-well, not very much," said the doctor, as he twirled his glasses on his tail.

Just then, who should come into the burrow but Mrs. Wren. She was very much surprised to see Uncle Wiggily lying on a bed of soft grass, with the doctor bending over him.

"What is the matter?" she asked.

"I have been shot," said Uncle Wiggily, "and the doctor cannot get the bullets out."

"Suppose you let me try," said Mrs. Wren. "I have a very sharp bill, and I think I can pull them out."

"Then you are a sort of a doctor," said Uncle Wiggily. "Go ahead, and see what you can do."

"Yes, do," urged Dr. Possum.

So the little brown bird put her beak in the holes in Uncle Wiggily's leg, where the bullets had gone in, and she pulled every one out. It hurt a little, but Uncle Wiggily did not make a fuss.

"There," said Mrs. Wren, "that is done."

Then Dr. Possum put some salve on the leg and bound it up, promising to come in next day to see how Uncle Wiggily was getting on.

"Did you find a nest-house?" asked Mamma Littletail of the bird.

"No," was the answer, "I think I shall have to stay with you another night, if you will let me. Perhaps I shall find a nest to-morrow."

So she stayed with the Littletail family another night, and to-morrow night I will tell you how she found a nest.

## Susie and Sammie Find a Nest

SAMMIE LITTLETAIL was up early the next morning. He had not slept very well, for Uncle Wiggily Longears had groaned very much because of the pain in his leg where he was shot. Sammie thought if he got up early, and went for some nice, fresh carrots for his uncle, it would make the old rabbit feel better.

While Sammie was digging up some carrots in a field not far from the burrow where he lived, he saw the same gray squirrel that had warned him about not going into the deer park.

"What are you doing now?" asked the squirrel. "It seems to me you are always doing something."

"I am digging carrots for Uncle Wiggily Longears that was shot," said Sammie.

"That is a very nice thing to do," the gray squirrel said. "You are a better boy rabbit than I thought you were."

"What are you doing here?" Sammie asked the squirrel.

"Me? Oh, I am moving into a new nest. I am getting ready for spring."

"A new nest!" exclaimed Sammie, and, all at once, he

thought of Mrs. Wren, who could not find a nest-house to live in. "What are you going to do with your old nest?" the little boy rabbit asked.

"Why leave it, to be sure. I never move my nest."

"Don't you want it any more?"

"Not in the least. I am through with it."

"May I have it?" asked Sammie, very politely.

"You? What can a rabbit do with a nest in a tree? They live in burrows."

"I know that," Sammie admitted. "I was not asking for myself," and then he told the squirrel about Mrs. Wren. "May she have your old nest?" he asked.

"Why, yes, if she likes it," the squirrel replied. "Only I am afraid she will find it rather large for such a little bird."

"I will hurry home and tell her," spoke Sammie.

"All right. Tell her she can move in any time she likes," called the gray squirrel after Sammie, who, filling his forepaws with carrots, started off toward home as fast as he could run. He found Mamma Littletail getting breakfast, and at once told her the good news. Then he told Mrs. Wren, who had gotten up early to get the early worm that always gets up before the alarm clock goes off.

"I will go and look at the nest at once," said the little bird. "I am very much obliged to you, Sammie. Where is it?"

"Susie and I will show you," spoke the little boy rabbit. "Only we cannot go all the way, because rabbits are not allowed in the deer park. But I can point it out to you."

So, after breakfast, Sammie and Susie started off. They ran on the ground and the little brown bird flew along over their heads. She went so much faster than they did that she had to stop every once in a while and

wait for them. But at last they got to the place where
they could see the deserted squirrel nest.

"There it is," said Sammie, pointing to it.

"So I observe," said the bird. "I will fly up and look at
it," which she did. She was gone some time, and when
she flew back to the ground, where Sammie and Susie
were waiting for her, the children asked:

"Did you like it?"

"I think it will do very well," replied Mrs. Wren. "It
is a little larger than I need, and there are not the
improvements I am used to. There is no hot and cold
water and no bathroom, but then I suppose I can bathe
in the brook, so that is no objection. There is no roof to
it, though."

"No roof?" repeated Sammie.

"No. You see, squirrels never have one such as I am
used to, but when my family comes from the South we
can build one. I will take the nest, and I hope you
bunnies will come to see me sometimes, when I am
settled, and have the carpets down."

"We can't climb trees," objected Susie.

"That's so—you can't," admitted Mrs. Wren. "Never
mind, I can fly down and see you. Now I think I will
begin to clean out the nest, for the squirrels have left a
lot of nutshells in it."

So she began to clean out the nest, and Susie and
Sammie started home. But, before they got there something happened, and what it was I will tell you, perhaps,
to-morrow night, if the rooster doesn't crow and wake
me up.

## Sammie Littletail Falls In

WHEN SAMMIE LITTLETAIL and his sister Susie went off toward the underground house, after they had shown Mrs. Wren where she could get the squirrel's old nest for a home, they felt very happy. They ran along, jumping over stones, leaping through the grass that was beginning to get very green, and had a jolly time.

"I wonder what makes me feel so good?" said Sammie to his sister. "It's just as if Christmas was coming, or something like that; yet it isn't. I don't know what it is."

"I know," spoke Susie, who was very wise for a little bunny-rabbit girl.

"What is it?" asked Sammie, as he paused to nibble at a sweet root that was sticking out of the ground.

"It is because we have been kind to somebody," went on Susie Littletail. "We did the little brown bird a kindness in showing her the squirrel's nest where she could go to housekeeping, and that's what makes us happy."

"Are you sure?" asked Sammie.

"Yes," said Susie; "I am," and she sat up on her hind legs and sniffed the air to see if there was any danger about. "You always feel good when you do any one a kindness," she went on. "Once I wanted to go out and

31

play, and I couldn't, because Nurse Fuzzy-Wuzzy was away and Mamma had a headache. So I stayed home and made Mamma some cabbage-leaf tea, and she felt better, and I was happy then, just as we are now."

"Well, maybe that's it," admitted Sammie Littletail. "I am glad Mrs. Wren has a nice home, anyhow. But I wouldn't like to live away up in a tree, would you?"

"No, indeed. I would be afraid when the wind blew and the nest shook."

"It is ever so much nicer underground in our burrow," continued Sammie.

"It certainly is," agreed Susie, "but I s'pose that a bird would not like that. They seem to want to be high up in the air. But I don't like it. Once I went away up on top of Farmer Tooker's woodpile, because his gray cat chased me, and when I looked down I was very dizzy, and it was not as high as a tree."

So the two bunny children hurried along, talking of many things, and, now and then, finding some nice sweet roots, or juicy leaves, which they ate. They paused every once in a while to look over the tops of the little hills to discover if any dogs or hunters or ferrets were in sight, for they did not want to be caught.

At length they came to a little brook that was not far from their home. Their edge of the stream had ice on it, for, though spring was approaching, the weather was still cold.

"Ah! There is some ice. I am going to have a slide!" Sammie shouted.

"You had better not!" cautioned his sister. "You might fall in."

"I will keep close to the shore," promised her brother, and he took a run and slid along the ice. "Come on!" he cried. "It's fun, Susie."

*"I've fallen in! Help me out!"*

The little bunny girl was just going to walk out on the ice, when Sammie, who had taken an extra long run, slid right off the ice and into the water.

"Oh! Oh, Susie!" he screamed. "I've fallen in! Help me out!"

"What shall I do?" asked his sister, and she stood up on her hind legs and waved her little paws in the air.

"Get a stick and let me grab it!" called Sammie. "But don't come too close, or you may fall in, too," for Sam-

mie was very fond of his sister, and did not want her to
get hurt. He clung to the edge of the ice, and shivered
in the cold water, while, with her teeth, Susie gnawed a
branch from a tree. The branch she held out to her
brother, who grasped it in his mouth and was soon
pulled up on shore. But, oh, how he shivered! And how
his fur was plastered down all over him, just like a cat
when it falls in the bathtub. But I hope none of you children ever put pussy in there.

"You must run home at once," said Susie, "and drink
some hot sassafras tea, so you won't take cold. Come
on, I'll run with you."

So they started off, running, leaping and bounding,
and by the time they got to their burrow, Sammie
was quite warm. Down the front door hole they
plunged, and, as soon as Sammie's mother saw him,
she cried out:

"Why, Sammie! You've been in swimming! Didn't I tell
you never to go in swimming?"

"I haven't been swimming, mother," said Sammie.

"Yes, you have; your hair is all wet," she answered.

Then Sammie told how he had fallen in. Uncle Wiggily
Longears, the old rabbit, heard him, and said he
guessed he would have to give Sammie and Susie some
lessons in swimming, and if you are good, I will tell you
to-morrow night what happened on that occasion.

## Jane Fuzzy-Wuzzy Gives a Lesson

UNCLE WIGGILY LONGEARS was a very wise old rabbit. He had lived so long, and had escaped so many dogs and hunters, year after year, that he knew about all a rabbit can know. Of course, that may not be so very much, but it was a good deal for Uncle Wiggily Longears. So the day after Sammie came home from having fallen in the brook the old rabbit got ready to give Sammie and Susie Littletail their swimming lesson.

"You will want to know how to get out of the water when you fall in," he said. "You come with me, and I will show you. It is not very cold out, and I will give you a short lesson."

"Be careful not to let them drown," cautioned Mamma Littletail.

"I will," promised Uncle Wiggily Longears, and he started from the burrow, followed by the two bunny children. But, just as their uncle got out of the front door he was seized with a sharp spasm of rheumatism.

"Oh! oh! oh, dear!" he cried three times, just like that.

"What is the matter?" asked Sammie.

"Rheumatism," answered Uncle Wiggily Longears, and he put his left front paw on his left hind leg. "I have it very bad. I don't believe I would dare go in the water with you children to-day. We will have to wait. Yet I don't like to, as you ought to learn to swim. I wonder if you could learn if I stood on the bank and told you what to do?"

"I think it would be much better if you could come into the water and show us," said Susie.

"Yes, of course it would," admitted Uncle Wiggily Longears. "Of course it would, my dear, only you see— ouch! Oh, me! Oh, my!" and poor Uncle Wiggily Longears wrinkled his nose and made it twinkle like a star on a frosty night, and he wiggled his ears to and fro. "Oh, that was a terrible sharp pain," he said. "I don't believe I'd better go, children. I'm awfully sorry——"

"Let me take the children and show them how to swim," said Nurse Jane Fuzzy-Wuzzy, who had just finished peeling the potatoes for dinner. She could peel them very nicely with her long, sharp front teeth, which were just like a chisel that a carpenter uses.

"Yes, I guess you could teach them," said Uncle Wiggily, as he rubbed his leg softly. "You are a much better swimmer than I am; but can you spare the time from the housework?"

You see, Jane Fuzzy-Wuzzy had to do all the housework for the Littletail family, but, as she was a very good muskrat, she was able to do it, and she often had time to spare, so she answered:

"Yes, I can just as well go as not, for I have the dinner on the stove, and Mr. Littletail will not be home to lunch. I will give the children a swimming lesson. It will not take long."

"Well," spoke Uncle Wiggily Longears, "I wish you would. I must go and get something for my rheumatism."

"You had better try a hot cabbage leaf," said Jane Fuzzy-Wuzzy. "I have heard that is good."

"I will," said the old rabbit, and he crawled back down into the burrow, while Susie and Sammie, with Nurse Jane Fuzzy-Wuzzy, went on to the brook.

The muskrat was a very good swimmer, indeed, and as soon as she reached the water she plunged in and swam about, to show Sammie and Susie how it ought to be done. She dived, and she shot across; she swam on her side, and in the ordinary way. In fact, she swam in a number of ways that you and I could not. At length she swam entirely under water for some distance, and the bunny children were afraid she was drowned, but she came up smiling, showing her sharp teeth, and explained that this was one of the ways she used to escape from dogs, boys and other enemies.

Then the nurse-muskrat gave the bunny children their lesson. She had little trouble in teaching them, as they learned quickly. She was just showing them how to float along with only the tip of the nose showing, in order to keep out of sight, when suddenly there was a noise on the bank.

No, it was not someone after the bunny rabbit children's clothes, for they had left them at home when they went to take a lesson. But it was a number of boys with a dog who were making the noise. As soon as the boys saw the rabbits and the muskrat they gathered up a lot of stones, and one boy cried out:

"Oh, look there! Two rabbits and a muskrat! Let's catch them, and sell their skins!"

"Oh, dear!" exclaimed Susie, who was very much frightened. "Whatever shall we do?"

"Don't be alarmed," said Nurse Jane Fuzzy-Wuzzy,

*It was a number of boys with a dog.*

calmly, as she started to swim down stream. "Just follow me; swim as I do, with only your nose out, and I will
save you." The boys ran along the bank, throwing
stones at the little creatures, and the dog barked, and
to-morrow night I will tell you how Sammie and Susie
got away and were saved by Jane Fuzzy-Wuzzy, that is
if you think you would care to hear the story.

## Sammie's and Susie's Terrible Time

YOU MAY be sure the two Littletail children were very much frightened when they were floating down the stream behind Nurse Jane Fuzzy-Wuzzy, with the boys on the bank throwing stones at them, and the dog barking as hard as he could bark.

"Sic the dog in the water after them," called one boy.

"Naw! This dog doesn't like water," said the boy who owned it. "We'll hit 'em with stones, and then poke 'em out with sticks."

Oh, how Sammie and Susie shuddered when they heard those words! They did not know Jane Fuzzy-Wuzzy was going to save them. The muskrat looked around to see how the children were swimming.

"Don't be afraid," she called, but of course the boys could not understand what she said. The dog could, being an animal and understanding animal talk, but the dog couldn't tell the boys.

"Don't be afraid," said the nurse. "Sammie, keep your head under more. Susie, strike out harder with your forepaws."

The two bunny children did as they were told. Just then a stone came very close to Jane Fuzzy-Wuzzy, and she went completely beneath the water.

39

"The muskrat's gone!" cried a boy.

"No," said another, "it can swim under water. But don't bother with the rabbits. They're little, and their fur isn't much good. Kill the muskrat, for we can get fifty cents for the skin."

"Oh, how mean boys are!" thought Susie Littletail. "To talk about selling poor Jane Fuzzy-Wuzzy's skin! Aren't they terrible!"

The boys now gave all their attention to throwing stones at the muskrat, but she was very wise, and kept under water as much as possible, so they could not hit her. They did not throw at Sammie or Susie. Presently Jane Fuzzy-Wuzzy swam backward under water and came up near Sammie. She put her sharp nose close to his ear and whispered:

"Down stream a little way is a burrow where I used to live. The front door is under water, but if you hold your breath you can dive down, get in and come up in the dry part. Then you can dig a way out in a field, and we can go home, and escape the boys."

Jane told the same thing to Susie, and, pretty soon, when they came to the place, the two bunny children took a long breath, and dived down under water. Sammie and Susie took hold of the long tail of Jane Fuzzy-Wuzzy to guide them in the dark, and, though it seemed a terrible thing not to breathe under water, the three suddenly found themselves in a little underground house, much like their own, where they could breathe again.

"Now we are safe!" exclaimed the muskrat. "Just dig a back door and you can get out."

So Sammie and Susie did so, and, pretty soon, they found themselves in a nice field, some distance back from the water. They could see the boys and their dog still watching near the bank to catch Jane Fuzzy-Wuzzy,

and the boys never knew how the muskrat and the rabbit children escaped.

"My! but that was exciting," said Sammie, when they
were on their way home.

"Indeed it was," agreed Susie. "I'm so frightened that
I have almost forgotten how to swim."

"It will all come back to you the next time you go in
the water," said Jane Fuzzy-Wuzzy. "But I must hurry
home now, or dinner will be late."

*The two bunny children dived down under water.*

They got to the burrow without anything more happening. Mamma Littletail and Uncle Wiggily Longears were much alarmed when told about the narrow escape.

"Those boys!" cried the old rabbit. "If I wasn't laid up with rheumatism, I'd show them!" and he snapped his teeth in quite a savage manner indeed, for a rabbit can get angry at times.

After dinner Mamma Littletail asked Sammie and Susie to go to the cabbage-field store for her, but, as Sammie wanted to stay home and make a whistle out of a carrot, Susie went alone. As she was walking along under a big tree, she heard a noise in the branches, and, looking up, she saw a number of squirrels. One was the squirrel who had given her old nest to Mrs. Wren. The little gray chaps were running about, seemingly much excited over something. Presently they all scampered down, and Susie saw that they had their mouths full of nuts. They put them on the ground in a little heap, and then the little bunny girl noticed that there was, nearby, an old stump, and it was set just like a table, with dried leaves for plates, and the tops of acorns for cups.

"What is going on here?" Susie asked the squirrel whom she knew.

"I am giving a party in honor of having moved into my new nest," said the squirrel. "Wouldn't you like to come?"

"Yes," said Susie very politely, "I would like very much to."

"Then," said the squirrel, "hop up on the stump, and I will get an extra plate for you." Susie did so. It was the first party she had ever attended, but I can't tell you what happened until to-morrow.

## Susie Goes to a Party

UP AND DOWN the big oak tree scampered the squirrels, bringing nuts and acorns from hollows, where they had been hidden all winter.

"Hey, Bushytail!" cried the squirrel whom Susie knew, addressing another who was on the ground at the foot of the stump, "bring up a big leaf."

"What do you want with a big leaf?" inquired the squirrel who was called Bushytail.

"Susie Littletail is going to stay to the party," replied the squirrel who was giving it, "and I want the leaf for a plate for her. She will need a large one."

Up the old stump climbed Bushytail with the leaf in his mouth, and he put it in a vacant place. The stump was quite large enough for the squirrels and rabbit to move about upon and still leave room for the table to be set. Susie saw the squirrels placing nut meats on the different plates and putting oak-leaf tea into the acorn cups. Suddenly the squirrel whom Susie knew and whose name was Mrs. Lightfoot, exclaimed:

"There! I never thought of that!"

"Thought of what?" asked Susie.

"Why, we haven't anything that you like to eat. You don't care for nuts, do you?"

"Not very much," answered Susie, who wanted to be polite, yet she still wanted to tell the truth.

"I thought so," spoke Mrs. Lightfoot. "Whatever shall I do? I've asked you to the party and now there is nothing that you like. It's too bad, for I want you to have a good time!"

"I—I could go to the cabbage-field store and get some leaves, and I could bring some carrots and eat them," suggested Susie.

"Yes, but it wouldn't be right to ask you to a party and then have you bring your own things to eat," objected Mrs. Lightfoot.

"That's what they do at surprise parties," went on Susie, who had heard Uncle Wiggily Longears tell of one he once attended. It was given by a chipmunk.

"Yes, but this isn't a surprise party," said Mrs. Lightfoot. "I don't know what to do."

"We can pretend it's a surprise party," went on Susie. "I know I was very much surprised when you asked me to come to it."

"Were you, indeed?" inquired the squirrel. "Then a surprise party it shall be. Listen!" she called to the other squirrels; "this is a surprise party for Susie Littletail."

"Humph! I don't call this a surprise," grumbled an old squirrel, whose tail had partly been shot off. But nobody minded him, as he was always grumbling. So Susie went and got some cabbage leaves and carrots, and brought them to the party. She had to eat them all alone, as the squirrels did not care much for such things. The only thing Susie could eat which the squirrels did was some ice cream, made with snow, maple syrup and hickory nuts ground up fine. This was very good.

Susie had a grand time at the party, and after the

hickory-nut ice cream and other good things had been eaten, she and the squirrels played "Ring Around the Old Oak Stump," which is something like "London Bridge" and "Ring Around the Rosy" mixed up together. It was lots of fun, and Susie almost forgot to go to the cabbage-field store. But she did go there, though it was just about to be closed up, and when she got home with the cabbage leaves for supper, she told about the surprise party. Then Sammie wished he had gone to the store, instead of remaining at home to make a whistle out of a carrot.

"I never had anything nice like that happen to me," said Sammie, in just the least bit of a grumbly voice. And, what do you think? The very next day something happened to Sammie, only it wasn't very nice. He was out walking in a field, when he met a big cat.

"Where do you live?" asked the cat, in quite a friendly voice.

"Over there," said Sammie, pointing toward the burrow.

"Can you take me there?" asked the cat, and she wiggled her whiskers and licked her nose with her tongue, for she was hungry.

"Yes, I'll show you," agreed Sammie, and he led the cat toward the burrow. Now, he did not know any better, for he did not stop to think that cats will eat rabbits. And the cat was just thinking how easily she had provided a good dinner for herself, when Jane Fuzzy-Wuzzy, who was peeping out of the front door of the burrow, saw pussy. The muskrat knew at once that the cat had come to eat the little rabbits and the big ones, too, and the only reason she did not eat Sammie was because she wanted more of a meal. So the nurse showed her sharp teeth, and the cat ran away. But she knew where the burrow was, and this was a bad thing,

*"Where do you live?" asked the cat.*

for she might come back again in the night, when Sammie and Susie were asleep.

"We must move away from here at once," said Uncle Wiggily Longears, when he heard about the cat. "We must find a new burrow or make one. Sammie, you acted very wrongly, but you did not mean to. Now, you must help us pack up to move." And to-morrow night, if all goes well, I shall tell you what happened when the Littletail family went to their new home.

## The Littletail Family Moves

DID YOU ever see a rabbit family move? No, I don't suppose you have, for not every one has had that chance. But the Littletail family, as I told you last night, had to move because a big cat had found out where their burrow was.

"I shall go out at once, and see if I can find a new place," said Uncle Wiggily Longears, after the excitement caused by Sammie bringing home the cat had calmed down. "We need a larger burrow, anyhow. I will find a nice one."

"Can you go out with your rheumatism?" asked Mamma Littletail. "You are very lame, you know. Perhaps you had better wait until Papa Littletail comes home to-night, and he will go."

"No, we must lose no time," said the uncle. "I can manage with my crutch, I guess."

So he started from the burrow, leaning heavily on a crutch Nurse Jane Fuzzy-Wuzzy had gnawed from a cornstalk.

"Be careful of the cat," cautioned Susie.

"Oh, no cat can catch me, even if I have the rheumatism very bad," said her uncle, and he limped away.

While he was gone, Nurse Jane Fuzzy-Wuzzy promised to keep a sharp lookout for that cat.

Uncle Wiggily Longears was gone for some time. When he returned to the burrow Papa Littletail had come back from where he worked in a carrot factory, which was a new position for him, and he had heard all the news.

"Well," he asked Uncle Wiggily, "did you find a new burrow?"

"Yes," answered the uncle, "I did. I will tell you all about it. I walked a long distance, and I met several friends of mine. I asked them about burrows, and they said the best ones were all taken. I was afraid you would have to dig a new one, until I met Mr. Groundhog, and he told me of one next to him, on the bank of a little pond. We can get it cheap, he said."

"Has it all improvements?" asked Mamma Littletail. "I want a good kitchen and a bathroom."

"It has everything," said the uncle. "It has three doors, and we can get in and out easily. It is near a cabbage-field and a turnip patch. We can bathe in the pond, so we don't need a bathroom."

"Where is it?" asked Papa Littletail. "I must be near the trolley, you know."

"It is not far from the cars," went on Uncle Wiggily Longears. "Have you ever heard of Eagle Rock?"

None of the family had.

"Well, it is not far from there," said Uncle Wiggily. "I went out on the rock, and my! what a view there was! I could see away over the big meadows, where some of your relatives live, Miss Fuzzy-Wuzzy, and then I could see something called New York."

"What's New York?" asked Susie Littletail.

"I don't know," answered her uncle promptly. "I imagine it must be something good to eat." But of course, children, you know how mistaken he was. Uncle Wiggily told more about his walk, and finally it was decided to take the new burrow, so the cat could not find them.

The next day the Littletail family moved. That is all they did, they just moved. They had no packing or unpacking to do, except that Sammie took the whistle he had made out of a carrot and Uncle Wiggily carried his cornstalk crutch. By noon they were all settled, and Jane Fuzzy-Wuzzy had cooked some of the new cabbage, which had been left in the field all winter, and also some turnips, which were piled under a lot of straw out-of-doors. She also found some potatoes, which she peeled with her sharp teeth.

*The next day the Littletail family moved.*

That afternoon, as' Sammie was hopping about his new home, he heard someone exclaim:

"Hello!"

"Hello," replied Sammie, who always wanted to be friendly.

"Where do you live?" the voice went on, and, all at once, Sammie thought of the cat.

"No, you don't!" he cried. "You can't fool me again. I know you!"

"Oh, do you?" asked the voice. "Well, seeing that I'm a stranger here, and you are too, I don't think that you know me."

Sammie looked on top of a clod of earth, whence the voice came, and saw a big frog.

"Oh, it's you, is it?" he asked faintly.

"Of course," replied the frog. "My name's Bully; what's yours?" Sammie told him. "Ever hear of me?" went on the frog, and when Sammie said he had not, the frog continued: "Well, let's see who can jump the farthest," and with that he began to get ready. Sammie, who was a very good jumper, did also, and just as they were about to see who was the better at it, there suddenly—— But there, I shall have to wait until to-morrow night to tell you what happened next.

## How the Water Got In

LET ME SEE, where did I leave off last night? Oh, I remember now, I was telling you about Sammie Littletail's new playmate, Bully, the frog, and how they were about to have a jumping contest, when something happened. This is what happened:

Bully was crouching down for a spring, when he suddenly looked up. This was not hard for him, as his eyes were nearly on top of his head, but Sammie had to get on his hind legs to peer upward properly. And this is what both of the little creatures saw: A big bird, with long legs and a very long bill, was standing on one leg right over the frog. The bird was looking intently at Bully.

"Come on!" cried the frog to the rabbit. "We must get away from here as quickly as we can."

"Why?" asked Sammie Littletail.

"Because," said Bully, "that bird will eat us. My father warned me never to stay near that bird. Let us go away at once."

"What sort of a bird is it?" asked Sammie, who now had no wish to jump. "I'm sure it can't be very harmful. The only birds that I have to look out for are owls, eagles and hawks, and it isn't any of them."

"No, I'm not one of them," spoke the bird with the long legs, snapping its bill as if sharpening it. "I'm a blue heron, that's what I am, though some folks think I'm a stork or a crane."

"Well," spoke Sammie, "you're not dangerous, are you?"

"Not for you," went on the blue heron, and he snapped his beak again, just like two knives being sharpened. "I came for that fellow," and the bird lowered the leg it had hidden under its feathers and pointed at the frog. "I came for you," the heron went on. "You're wanted at once. What's your name?"

Sammie Littletail thought the bird might have asked the frog's name first before saying that Bully was wanted, but the bird did not seem to consider this.

"What's your name?" the long-legged bird asked again.

"Bully," answered the frog, in a trembling, croaking voice.

"Humph!" exclaimed the heron. "That's a good name. Mine is Billy. Bully and Billy go well together. I'm called Billy because I have such a long bill, you see," the heron explained to Sammie Littletail. "But enough of this. I've come for you, Bully. I'm hungry. I'm going to eat you. That's why you're wanted at once and immediate."

"I—I think there's some mistake," faltered Bully.

"No mistake at all," snapped the heron. "It's in all the books. Cranes, storks and herons always eat frogs, mice and-so-forth. I never ate any and-so-forth, but I imagine it must be very nice. At any rate, I'm going to eat you!" and he snapped his bill like three knives being sharpened.

"Oh, are you?" cried Bully, the frog, and he suddenly gave a great jump, greater even than that which the Jumping Frog that Mark Twain wrote about gave, and into the pond he plunged, and went right to the bottom. Now, what do you think about that? Yes, sir, he went right to the bottom, where the blue heron couldn't get him, and then he called up, in a voice which sounded very hoarse because it came from so far under water:

"Ha! Who got left?"

"I suppose he means me," spoke the heron to Sammie, and the bird, very much annoyed, fanned itself with its long leg. "I don't believe that's fair," the heron went on. "It's in all the books," and then, with a great flapping of wings, the tall creature flew away, and Bully, the frog, came out.

"You had a narrow escape," said Sammie.

*Into the pond he plunged.*

"Oh, I'm used to that," replied the frog. "Now, let's practice jumping."

Which they did, only the frog always jumped into the water and Sammie remained on dry land, so they never could tell who was the best at it. Then they played other games, and became very good friends. The frog pond was very near the new burrow where Sammie lived, and the two used to meet quite often. One day the frog said:

"I think it would be very nice if you would dig a way from your burrow to my pond. Then, when it rained, I could come to see you without getting wet, and you could come to see me."

"That is a fine idea," declared Sammie. "I'll do it."

So, without saying anything to his mother or sister or Uncle Wiggily Longears, Sammie began to dig under ground to reach the pond. It took him some time, but at last he came out just above the top of the water, near where Bully lived.

"This is great!" cried the frog, as he looked in the hole. "Now when it rains we will not get wet."

And, what do you think! It rained that very night. It rained so hard that the pond rose higher and higher, until the water began to run in the hole Sammie had dug. It awakened the Littletail family in the middle of the night, and when Uncle Wiggily Longears saw the water creeping nearer and nearer to him, and felt the rheumatism worse than ever, he cried out:

"A flood! A flood! We must swim out, or we shall all be drowned." Now you will have to be patient until to-morrow night to hear what took place. But they were not drowned; I'll tell you that much.

## Sammie and Susie at the Circus

O F COURSE, you remember how Sammie Littletail dug a tunnel from the burrow to the pond, and how the water came in. Of course. Well, Nurse Jane Fuzzy-Wuzzy made a raft of cornstalks, and on this the whole rabbit family floated out of the burrow. Bully, the frog, who was a playmate of Sammie's, helped them. They had to go right out into the rain, and it was not very pleasant.

"Whatever are we going to do?" asked Mamma Littletail, but she did not scold Sammie for digging the tunnel and making all the trouble.

"Yes, we must get in out of the wet, or my rheumatism will be so bad I shall not be able to walk," complained Uncle Wiggily Longears.

"I know what we can do," proposed the muskrat nurse.

"What?" asked Susie Littletail.

"We can ask Mr. Groundhog to let us stay all night in his burrow," suggested the nurse. "I'm sure he will let us, for he has plenty of room."

Mr. Groundhog, who was an elderly creature, very fond of sleep in the winter, welcomed the rabbits to his burrow, and there they stayed out of the rain. In the morning the sun was shining brightly, and before very long the water all dried out of the bunnies' underground house, so that they could go back in it.

One day, about a week after this, when Uncle Wiggily Longears was out walking with Sammie and Susie, going quite slowly, because he was a trifle lame from rheumatism, Bully, the frog, came hopping up to them.

"Are you going to the circus?" he asked.

"Circus? What circus?" asked Sammie, who was interested very quickly, you may be sure.

"Why, the animal circus that is always held in the woods every spring. They do all sorts of queer things to get ready for the summer. I'm going. It's lots of fun. Better come."

"I haven't seen any circus posters up," remarked Susie.

"Of course not," answered Bully. "The animals never put them up, because they don't want a lot of people coming to look on and bother them. Don't you want to come? It's not very far."

"But we have no one to take us," spoke Susie.

"Yes, you have!" exclaimed Uncle Wiggily Longears quickly. "I will take you myself. It would never do for you children to go to a circus alone. I will take you."

"But your rheumatism is so bad you can hardly walk," objected Susie. "Besides, it will be worse if you sit in the woods."

"Never mind about that," answered the uncle bravely. "I'll manage to stand it. I am determined you children shall not go to that circus alone. Of course, I don't care anything about a circus myself, but I must take care of you," and the elderly rabbit looked very brave, though the pain of his rheumatism was quite bad.

"My father is going to hop over three stumps," said

*Then the performance began.*

Bully, the frog, quite proudly. "Come on, or we may
be late."

So Uncle Wiggily took Sammie and Susie to the animal circus, and Bully, the frog, went also. He had a free
ticket, because his father was one of the performers.
They had reserved seats on big toadstools, though
Bully said they ought to be called frogstools, as frogs
used them more than toads did.

Then the performance began, after the birds had
sung an opening chorus. The bunny children had a jolly
time. They saw some pigeons give airship exhibitions

that were better than any flying machines you ever heard of. They watched the snakes make hoops of themselves, through which jumped squirrels and rabbits. It was so exciting that Uncle Wiggily Longears clapped his paws as hard as he could. Then Dr. Possum, who was not very busy taking care of sick people that day, hung downward from a limb by his tail ever so long, but when Bully's papa jumped over three big stumps at once, without so much as touching one— well, you should have heard the clapping and shouting then! Best of all, Sammie and Susie liked the baby deer, who stood up on his hind legs and danced, while a crow whistled. It was so exciting that Sammie and Susie almost forgot to eat the candy-covered carrots and the molasses-cabbage which their uncle bought for them. It was the best time they had ever remembered, and they talked of nothing else on their way home. Even Uncle Wiggily's rheumatism seemed better.

Now, listen, to-morrow night's story is going to be about—let me see—Oh! on second thought I believe there are enough stories in this book, and, if you would like to read some more I'll have to put them in another. Now, good-bye for a little while, dear children.

THE END